THE AMULET
OF AVANTIA

EQUINUS
THE
SPIRIT HOUSE

*With special thanks to Jan Burchett
and Sara Vogler*

For Timotej Torak, with all good wishes

www.beastquest.co.uk

ORCHARD BOOKS
338 Euston Road, London NW1 3BH
Orchard Books Australia
Level 17/207 Kent St, Sydney, NSW 2000

A Paperback Original
First published in Great Britain in 2009

Beast Quest is a registered trademark of Working Partners Limited
Series created by Working Partners Limited, London

Text © Working Partners Limited 2009
Cover illustration by Steve Sims © Orchard Books 2009
Inside illustrations by Brian@KJA-artists.com © Orchard Books

A CIP catalogue record for this book is available from
the British Library.

ISBN 978 1 40830 377 1

3 5 7 9 10 8 6 4

Printed in the UK by CPI Bookmarque, Croydon, CR0 4TD

The paper and board used in this paperback are natural recyclable
products made from wood grown in sustainable forests. The
manufacturing processes conform to the environmental regulations of
the country of origin.

Orchard Books is a division of Hachette Children's Books,
an Hachette UK company.

www.hachette.co.uk

EQUINUS
THE
SPIRIT HORSE

BY ADAM BLADE

ORCHARD BOOKS

The Forbidden Land

THE DEAD VALLEY

THE DEAD JUNGLE

THE DARK WOOD

THE DEAD PEAKS

All hail, fellow followers of the Quest.

We have not met before, but like you, I have been watching Tom's adventures with a close eye. Do you know who I am? Have you heard of Taladon the Swift, Master of the Beasts? I have returned – just in time for my son, Tom, to save me from a fate worse than death. The evil wizard, Malvel, has stolen something precious from me, and until Tom is able to complete another Quest, I cannot be returned to full life. I must wait between worlds, neither human nor ghost. I am half the man I once was and only Tom can return me to my former glory.

Will Tom have the strength of heart to help his father? This new Quest would test even the most determined hero. And there may be a heavy price for my son to pay if he defeats six more Beasts...

All I can do is hope – that Tom is successful and that I will one day be returned to full strength. Will you put your power behind Tom and wish him well? I know I can count on my son – can I count on you, too? Not a moment can be wasted. As this latest Quest unfolds, much rides upon it.

We must all be brave.

Taladon

PROLOGUE

"Now it's your turn to give me a dare!" Jak told his friend, Flint.

The boys were playing on the edge of their village. The sun had almost set over Errinel and heavy shadows were creeping across the ground. The sky was the colour of a deep purple bruise, but the approaching darkness just made their game of dare even more exciting.

Flint looked around and Jak saw his eyes light up as he pointed towards some trees in a nearby field.

"Dare you to pinch an apple from Farmer Grindall's orchard," said Flint.

"No problem!" Jak vaulted over a wooden fence, strolled into the orchard and climbed up the tallest apple tree. He'd show Flint he wasn't scared – even though grumpy old Farmer Grindall would chase him away with a stick if he saw him.

As he reached the top branch, he had a good view of the road that led away from the village and ran alongside the boundary of Avantia, King Hugo's realm. The boundary was marked by a high forbidding wall, into which was set an old iron gate. Even from his position in the tree, Jak couldn't see over it.

Beyond the wall was the Forbidden Land. Jak knew that no one ever went there. The other villagers wouldn't even talk about it. But looking at the sinister black wall gave him an idea for the best dare ever!

He plucked an apple, swung down from the tree and jumped back over the fence.

"You win that one," admitted Flint, as Jak tossed him the apple.

"Now here's your next dare," said Jak. "It's so frightening, I bet you won't do it."

"Nothing's too frightening for me!" Flint said confidently.

"I dare you to go into the Forbidden Land!" challenged Jak. He folded his arms, sure that his friend would admit defeat. *I wonder which forfeit I should give him*, he thought.

But Flint didn't say a word. Instead,

he strode down the road to the gate in the wall.

Jak ran after him, his heart beating fast. "You don't have to do it," he called. "It was just a joke."

"I never say no to a dare," said Flint, and he grasped the ironwork and began to climb.

"Then I'm coming with you." The gate was rusty and felt unstable beneath Jak's grip as he scrambled up it. But he couldn't let his friend go alone.

The boys were soon sitting astride the gate, staring in amazement at the sight before them. The Forbidden Land was grey as far as the eye could see. The ground was covered with a thick layer of dust and the only trees that grew nearby were blackened and gnarled.

"It's horrible!" Flint said with a gasp.

"Everything is so dead-looking," murmured Jak in reply.

They slid to the ground of the Forbidden Land and walked slowly away from the gate. Their boots left deep prints in the ash-like powder. Jak saw his friend shiver.

"We've done the dare," Flint said. His voice sounded odd and flat in this strange place, and the gate suddenly seemed far away. "Let's get back."

Jak nodded, but just then he spotted something on the horizon. "What's that?"

Flint followed his gaze. "It looks like a dust cloud." His face suddenly creased with worry and he glanced down at his feet. "Can you feel the ground moving?"

Jak could. The grey earth beneath their feet was vibrating and sending shudders up their legs.

"Something's coming," he whispered. The boys stood transfixed as the cloud of dust got nearer and the vibrations coming from the ground became stronger.

"It's a horse!" Flint exclaimed, peering into the distance. "And it's big."

Jak looked hard. His friend was right. He could just make out a glint of hooves and realised that the hoofbeats must be causing the vibrations. He caught a glimpse of a man sitting tall in the saddle. "I wonder who the rider is," he said as the horse got closer. "No, wait..."

With rising horror, he saw that the man's body was joined to the horse.

It was some kind of Beast – part man, part horse. But the Beasts didn't exist, did they? They were just made-up stories of Avantia that Jak repeated when he wanted to scare his little brother.

The Beast suddenly became transparent and Jak felt his jaw drop open in shock.

"I can see right through him," gasped Flint, and he swallowed nervously. "It's a ghost. And it's coming straight for us!"

Jak and Flint dashed for the gate, their feet churning up the grey dust. The Beast was getting closer, but the boys were fast runners. *We're going to make it*, Jak thought with relief. However, just as they got to the wall, Flint tripped and fell sprawling into the dust.

Jak quickly helped him stand, but above their heads came an almighty roar. The friends looked up. The Beast, solid once again, was on top of them and rearing up on its hind legs, ready to crush them. Jak gazed at the monster and saw an expression of joy and delight etched onto its skull-like face.

The boys were paralysed with fear and screamed as the terrifying Beast lunged down. Jak felt an icy cold sweep over his whole body, and gasped as he realised that the Beast had turned ghostly again and somehow passed straight through him. Tears of despair trickled down Jak's face as he felt something being torn from him. He forced himself to look at Flint. His friend stood pale and expressionless.

With his last thought, Jak knew what had happened to them both. The Beasts were real, after all. And although they hadn't been crushed to death, their fate was something far worse. The Beast had taken their life force.

CHAPTER ONE

A NEW DANGER

Tom made his way through the mine tunnels with Elenna close by his side. He could see daylight ahead. Only moments before, they had defeated Nixa the death-bringer, one of Malvel's evil Ghost Beasts. He was glad to be leaving the dark and the memories of the shape-shifter behind.

"We'll soon be out of here,"

declared Elenna, tightening the coil of rope round her waist. "And the sooner the better."

"It was a hard Quest," said Tom. "But we won in the end."

"And we've got back the first piece of the amulet for your father," said Elenna with a grin. I know there are five more to go, but it's a good start."

"My father looked stronger already when he appeared to us just now, didn't he?" Tom said eagerly.

Elenna nodded.

Tom felt a surge of happiness. He had grown up not knowing whether his father, Taladon, was alive or dead, but two days ago Tom had come face to face with him. He'd discovered that his father was a ghost, stranded between the real world and the spirit realm. Malvel's evil magic had done this, and the only way to make Taladon flesh and blood again was to locate the six pieces of the Amulet of Avantia and fit them all together. This was Tom's Quest, but it would not be easy to recover the amulet fragments. Each piece was guarded by one of Malvel's Ghost Beasts.

Tom touched the first fragment of the amulet, which hung from the leather cord round his neck. Taladon had told them that the second piece was guarded by Equinus the Spirit Horse.

"Father said Equinus would be a dangerous foe," Tom commented. "But we won't let that stop us."

"No, we won't," Elenna said determinedly. "Look, we're leaving the mines at last!" They ran out of the tunnel.

As they blinked in the sunlight, they heard a friendly whinny and a happy bark. Storm, Tom's stallion, and Silver, Elenna's wolf, came charging over to them.

"Thank you for waiting so patiently," Tom said to Storm, as he stroked the horse's glossy black neck.

"I think they're glad to see us!" Elenna laughed. Silver was jumping round her in circles, barking excitedly.

"Now the team's all together, we can start our next Quest." Tom held out his hand. "Map," he called.

The air in front of them shimmered and the map that Aduro had given to Tom materialised. They needed to fight Ghost Beasts – so the map itself was ghostly. It hung in the air before them, showing the whole of the dusty, grey Forbidden Land.

"We're here." Elenna pointed to the rocky mouth of the mine on the map.

"And that's the way we must go!" exclaimed Tom, as a glowing path appeared that led in a straight line across the map and into a tangled knot of trees. "To that forest in the east." He stared at the picture. The trees looked dark and forbidding. He knew that somewhere among those trunks lurked Equinus.

Tom flicked open the brass lid of the compass his father had given him. He did not need to look to remember the words inscribed on its underside: *For My Son*. They always filled him with a warm glow.

There were two points on the compass, *Destiny* and *Danger*. As Tom held the instrument out towards the forest, the needle swung towards *Destiny*. "We have a long journey ahead of us," he said. "It'll be quicker if we ride." He swung up onto Storm's back and held out a hand to Elenna.

"The beginning of another adventure!" cried Elenna, as she climbed up behind him. She sounded excited, but Tom could sense that she had the same fears as he did. The two friends had already met many fearsome and terrifying Beasts on their Quests.

What new terrors awaited them now?

CHAPTER TWO

THROUGH THE DEAD LAND

"I wonder what Equinus will be like?" said Elenna as they cantered along, Silver bounding eagerly at their heels. They had travelled a long way from the mine, but the land was still just as flat and grey in all directions.

"Equinus can't be worse than Nixa," Tom answered. "She was one of the most devious Beasts we've ever met."

He peered ahead across the plain. On a previous Quest, Tom had collected the pieces of a suit of magical golden armour, which Malvel had stolen. The suit was now safely back in King Hugo's palace, but Tom still had its magical powers. He called on the power from the golden helmet – the ability to see incredible distances. However, Tom couldn't yet see any sign of the forest they were heading for, just more dull grey land with one or two ashen bushes and solitary trees here and there.

"This isn't the most cheerful place we've ever been," said Elenna. "Even the sunshine doesn't feel warm."

Tom looked up. The sky was bright,

but its light was cold and dead, and the air was heavy with a stale, musty smell.

"I don't think we've ever been anywhere as desolate," he said. "Gorgonia was frightening, but this is just so…empty."

"Nothing but dust," agreed Elenna. "Poor Silver's getting covered in it." She leant down to her pet wolf. "Sorry, boy. Wish you could ride with us, but there's not enough room!"

Silver sneezed and shook himself, throwing out dusty grey clouds all around him.

They rode on.

"I can see treetops!" Tom said suddenly. He reined in Storm and looked intently into the distance. "It must be the forest."

"At last!" exclaimed Elenna.

his legs and the stallion snorted and set off at a gallop. Silver bounded ahead.

But as they neared the trees, Storm's pace slowed to a trot and Silver hung back. Tom tried urging Storm to go faster, but the stallion would only take anxious steps forward, glancing nervously to the left and right. Tom felt Elenna's grip tighten round his waist. She was apprehensive as well. He put his hand to his sword. He knew he must be strong. If there was a Beast waiting for them here, when might it appear? Was Equinus hiding in the shelter of the trees?

As if in answer to Tom's thoughts, an ear-piercing scream split the air.

CHAPTER THREE

CHARGE OF THE GHOST BEAST

Storm reared up at the terrifying sound, his front hooves flying. Tom and Elenna clung on as the stallion bucked and twisted in terror.

Tom vaulted quickly out of the saddle. "Hold on tight!" he shouted to Elenna. "I'll try to calm him down." Dodging the flailing hooves, he leapt at Storm's bridle and gripped it hard.

The stallion's nostrils were flared and his flanks heaved. It took all of Tom's strength to hold on to the terrified horse, and he could see that Elenna was only just managing to remain seated. Tom stroked Storm's head and spoke to him soothingly, and almost instantly the horse began to settle. Elenna slipped from the stallion's back, looking stunned.

"Thanks, Tom," she said. Silver crept over to her, his belly close to the ground. Hackles rising, he cowered at her feet, growling softly.

"What could have made that noise?" said Elenna with a shiver. "It sounded as if it was coming from the trees."

"I don't know," answered Tom. "But whatever it is, we must be ready for it."

Just then Elenna gave a cry of warning as a huge shape, shrouded in a cloud of dust, came crashing out of the trees.

Tom looked more closely. It was a Beast. It had a man's torso fixed to the body of a horse, and was heading straight for them. "Equinus!" Tom breathed.

"He's just like Tagus!" Elenna said. "But much bigger."

As the cloud of dust parted, Tom could see the Beast more clearly. The sight made his blood run cold. Even from this distance, the evil flashing in Equinus's blazing eyes was visible. The Beast's lank brown hair lashed the air behind him and his hideous skeletal face was parched dry, like the land all around them.

Elenna put a reassuring hand on Silver's back. He whimpered, pressing hard against her leg. Meanwhile, Tom struggled to hold on to Storm's bridle – the terrified stallion was tossing his head and trying to pull away.

Tom felt the ground vibrating beneath his feet as the Beast galloped towards them, churning up great clouds of dust. The force of his pounding hooves broke apart the dry

earth, and cracks snaked towards
them and spread out around
their feet.

"Get behind me, Elenna," Tom
urged, as he gave her Storm's reins
and drew his sword.

He frowned as he saw that the
Beast's form was changing. One
minute Equinus was solid, his skin
coloured like a sickly bruise, but the
next Tom could see the forest through
his body. Tom realised that Equinus
had the ability to take both solid and
ghostly forms, just like Nixa – which
made him a most dangerous enemy.

As the Beast drew closer, Tom saw
his heart throbbing in his chest. He
felt a new thrill of horror run through
him. This was no ordinary heart. It
was as black as night.

Tom knew that he must not let his

friends face such a foe. Controlling his own rising fear, he held up his wooden shield. It gleamed with the six tokens given to him by the good Beasts of Avantia. Each token had helped protect him on his Quests, and thinking of them gave him the courage he needed now.

"While there is blood in my veins, I will not fail in my Quest!" he shouted. Slashing the sword fiercely above his head, he leapt forwards to meet the Beast. But as he charged, he realised that he was not alone. Silver was running alongside him, barking wildly, and Elenna was on his other side, bow and arrow ready in her hands. Tom's heart soared as he caught sight of his brave stallion galloping ahead. They had all come to help him!

Equinus had taken his solid form
again. His mighty bulk reared up in
front of Tom. Gripping his sword
tightly in both hands, Tom cut a great
arc through the air just as Equinus
came down towards him. The Beast
dodged the sword and landed with a

clattering of hooves. Equinus turned to face him again. There was a sudden, terrible silence. The Beast's blazing eyes bore into Tom's and one of his giant hooves pawed the ground, like a bull ready to charge.

Slowly they began to circle each other. Sword at the ready, Tom kept his eyes fixed on his enemy. Looking at the Beast's heaving chest and massive muscles, Tom could see that strength alone would not be enough to defeat him. He knew that Elenna was standing a little way back, with Storm and Silver at her side, but he sensed that even the four of them would be no match for this mighty enemy.

Equinus's eyes were blood-red with evil hatred and he tossed his head angrily from side to side. Suddenly he lunged forwards and Tom only just managed to beat him back with fierce thrusts from his sword. Tom pressed his advantage, but caught his foot on a root, stumbled and fell. The Beast reared up, foam flying from his snarling lips.

Elenna cried out in alarm and Tom saw her shoot an arrow at the flank of the Beast. It bounced off harmlessly, but it was enough to distract Equinus. The Beast now turned to face Elenna.

Tom leapt to his feet. He knew he had to act quickly. This was his chance to plunge his sword deep into the black heart of the Beast.

He sized up his enemy. Equinus was tall, so Tom got ready to use the magic jumping ability from the golden armour, which would allow

him to leap up and strike the Beast.
He crouched, ready to spring,
waiting to feel the surge of strength
that usually coursed through his legs.
But nothing happened! He tried
again. Nothing.

Equinus still had his eyes fixed on
Elenna, Storm and Silver. His thin
lips parted in a horrible snarl and he
let out a sharp cry of evil laughter.
He reared up and began to gallop
towards Tom's friends.

"No!" Tom yelled at the top of his
voice. Fury surged through his veins.
He was not going to let his friends be
hurt – or worse. Tom started to run.

Elenna fired off more arrows, but
Equinus would not be halted.
Instead he slightly changed his
direction and charged straight
towards Storm. The stallion seemed

transfixed with terror and did not move.

Tom ran even faster. Equinus reared up, and Tom could see that the Beast was about to crush poor Storm. Elenna gave a shriek of fear as she joined Tom in the desperate dash towards the stallion. But they were too late. Equinus gave a cruel cry of mocking laughter as he crashed down on top of Storm.

CHAPTER FOUR

TOM'S CHOICE

"Storm!" shouted Tom, his voice hoarse. Suddenly he saw the Beast flicker and change into his ghostly form, and instead of crushing Storm he charged straight through him. The air around the horse and Beast shuddered, giving off a harsh silver light. Tom felt the force of it pushing him backwards. Silver bowed his head and Elenna held up her hands to

shield herself from the blazing glare.
Tom saw Storm drop to his knees.

Equinus veered round and Tom saw
that his evil black heart had swelled
in his chest and pounded more
strongly than before. The Beast gave
a shriek of triumph, and every angle
on his mocking skeletal face stood
out sharp and cruel. Then he
galloped off towards the forest,
churning the dust around him as he
went. In an instant he had vanished.

Tom turned back to Storm. He could see that his friend was taking in deep, shuddering breaths. He was still alive! Tom raced over to him, with Elenna close behind. But even before Tom reached Storm, he knew that something was wrong. The stallion was making no effort to stand up. Tom took the horse's bridle and helped him to his feet. He stroked him soothingly, but Storm stood silently and seemed unable to take a step forwards. Even when Tom flung his arms round Storm's neck, the black stallion made no sign that he recognised his friend.

"Storm, it's me," whispered Tom, stroking the horse's shoulder. "It's OK. The Beast has gone. You're safe."

"I think something's happened to him, Tom," said Elenna, looking distressed. "His eyes are…strange."

Tom gazed deeply into Storm's brown eyes. "They're dead!" he said with a gasp. "It's like looking at a stone carving. Oh, Storm, I've failed you. What has Equinus done?"

Elenna buried her face in Storm's mane. Silver whined at her feet.

"I think I can explain," said a voice.

Tom and Elenna whirled round at the sound. A soft golden glow filled the air and a vision of Taladon appeared. He stared gravely at them and then looked at Storm, who was still gazing sightlessly into the distance.

"Father! Tell me quickly!" said Tom. "What's happened to Storm?"

Taladon bowed his head in sorrow. "Equinus does not kill. He does something even more evil. He feeds

on the spirits of other creatures and
leaves them to a dismal, cheerless life
forever after. He has taken Storm's
spirit. I am so sorry. I did not think
this would happen."

Tom remembered how Equinus's
heart had grown larger after his
attack on Storm. Now he understood.

It had swelled thanks to Storm's stolen life force. Suddenly he was full of rage – and not just against Equinus. He was boiling with anger towards his father, too. "If you knew all about this, why didn't you tell me it could happen?" he shouted at him, fists clenched. "I would never have exposed my friends to such danger."

"You are right, my son," said Taladon quietly. "I knew about the power of Equinus, and I should have warned you."

"Then you have done a terrible thing!" Tom almost choked on the words.

Elenna took his arm. "Don't, Tom," she pleaded. "I'm sure Taladon can explain."

"I hope so, Elenna," Tom's father said in the same quiet tone. "You see,

I was convinced that you'd be able
to use one of your many powers
to overcome Equinus, but I was
wrong to think that. I was wrong
to expect that."

Tom stared hard at his father.
"What do you mean?"

"It weakens me each time I appear
to you like this. But I must show you
something." Taladon held out his
hand and made a movement in the
air. A vision immediately materialised
in front of Tom and Elenna. Tom
started in surprise. There before them
was an image of the rearing Equinus.
Silver gave a low growl and stood in
front of Elenna, as if to protect her.

"Look carefully," Taladon told Tom.
"This will help you understand."

As he spoke, Tom himself appeared
in the vision. Now Tom realised what

his father was showing him. It was
the struggle he had just had with
Equinus. He saw himself brandishing
his sword and trying to leap at the
Beast's black heart. It filled him with
horror to relive the terrible moment:
to see himself crouched ready for
the giant leap – and then finding
that he was unable to do it. A feeling
of utter helplessness flooded over
him again, as in the vision he saw
Equinus charge at Storm and pass
through him.

Taladon raised a hand and the vision
was gone. Elenna had tears running
down her face. She wiped them away,
as if she didn't want anyone to see.
Tom swallowed down his own grief
for the noble stallion who was lost to
him forever. What good were his
Quests without Storm by his side?

"I failed," said Tom brokenly.
"Why are you reminding me of it?"

Taladon shook his head. "It was
not your failure, my son," he said,
looking kindly at him. "Something
happened that you could not
overcome."

Tom shot a questioning glance at
his father.

"Let me explain," Taladon continued.
"You took on the task of finding
the six pieces of my amulet – and
I cannot tell you how proud I am
that you were brave enough to
accept the challenge. But I would not
have let you set out if I had known
the true price of your Quest." He
paused for a moment. "You see, with
each piece of amulet that you
recover, one of the magical powers
granted to you by the golden armour

will return to its true master…me. The armour was once mine and its powers are returning my strength."

"That's why you couldn't leap!" exclaimed Elenna. "The moment we defeated Nixa and won back the first piece of amulet, the power from your golden boots must have returned to Taladon."

Tom's father nodded. "Now, son, I need to ask you a question, and I want you to think very seriously before you answer it." He looked intently at Tom. "I would not for the world put you and your companions in more peril. And there will surely be danger ahead of you. Do you wish to continue with this Quest?"

Tom looked deep into his father's eyes. If he gave up now, Taladon would be a ghost forever. If he was to become flesh and blood again, the six pieces of the amulet must be recovered. And only Tom could do that. He raised his sword high in the air. "While there is blood in my veins, I will complete this Quest!"

CHAPTER FIVE

TIME IS RUNNING OUT

"I knew you wouldn't give up, Tom," said Taladon with a smile.

As he spoke, the air around him seemed to glow brightly, sending its warmth deep into Tom's heart. His father was proud of him, and that was enough. But then a stab of pain shot through him as he remembered Storm, who was now nothing but an empty shell, refusing to move. He would have no choice but to leave his poor horse behind while he completed the Quest.

As if he knew what Tom was thinking, Taladon gave his reply briskly.

"All is not lost. There is still time to save your friend."

"But how?" Tom asked desperately. He wanted to hold on to his father and keep his comforting image with him throughout his Quest, but he knew it was impossible.

"A tiny piece of Storm's life force remains." Taladon's voice was a distant whisper now. "If you defeat Equinus soon, Storm will get his spirit back. If you fail, he will be lifeless forever."

Tom looked at Elenna with sudden hope. Elenna's eyes were gleaming with determination.

"We're going to save Storm!" he vowed.

"We just need to find a way to defeat that horrible Beast," answered Elenna.

"We've never failed before," declared Tom. "And we won't this time. But we need help."

He whirled round to his father, only to find that the vision was gone. Tom and Elenna were alone.

As Tom's head hung in disappointment, Elenna took him by the shoulders. "Tom, you can do this!" she urged him. "For your father – and for Storm."

Tom nodded gravely. "Storm must stay here," he said firmly. "He can't defend himself without his life force. If he comes with us he'll be in terrible danger."

He gathered Storm's reins to tie them to a nearby oak tree. Its bark was pale and its leaves thin and papery. As Tom tossed the reins over a low branch, acorns tumbled around him and crumbled to dust. Elenna came to his side, with Silver at her heels.

"I'll set Silver to guard him." She bent down and patted his thick coat. "You must stay here and look after Storm," she told the wolf. "We will be back as soon as we can."

Silver seemed to understand. He gave the stallion a friendly nudge and then took a bold stance next to him.

"He won't let us down," Elenna smiled.

Silver gave Elenna's hand an eager lick, but Storm stood motionless as the two friends said goodbye to him. Tom wrenched his gaze away from his horse and turned resolutely towards the dreaded forest.

Suddenly Elenna stopped in her tracks. "Tom!" she cried. "Those trees ahead don't look like they're part of an ordinary forest. I think it's a rainforest."

Tom halted as well. He had been so busy worrying about Storm that he hadn't paid attention to how the environment was changing. He took in the dense tangle of huge leaves and creepers.

"Well, that's the way Equinus went, so that's the way we're going," he declared.

They strode boldly into the jungle.
The trunks were close together, their
thick branches stretching towards the
sky as if they were fighting each
other for the light. The trees were
suffocated with vines and ivy.
Everything was parched and grey.

"We've never seen a jungle quite
like this," Elenna said, reaching out

to push aside a creeper. It turned to powder at her touch. "It's all dead," she said, coughing in the dusty air. "Just like the rest of the Forbidden Land."

Tom strode into the tangle of plants, crushing the knee-high undergrowth as he went. His shoulder brushed against a massive tree trunk and bark peeled away.

"Urgh!" exclaimed Elenna, following in his wake, as they drove deeper into the jungle. "This ash is clinging to my legs. It's horrible!"

"The air is thick with it," agreed Tom. "It's hard to even breathe. I just hope this is the right path."

As if in answer, Tom's ghostly map appeared in front of them, glowing in the half-light that filtered through the dense foliage. There on the map was the rainforest, and deep within the trees was a tiny image of Equinus, with a path leading straight to him.

"It looks as if we've just got to keep going," said Elenna grimly, as the map faded. "It won't be long before we find him – or he finds us..."

"I hope he does seek us out. The

sooner we find him, the sooner we can defeat him," said Tom. "We need to save Storm."

"We'll save him. Equinus doesn't stand a chance against the both of us," declared Elenna.

Tom threw her a look of gratitude. Elenna's friendship was the best gift he had. He struck out again through the undergrowth, with Elenna a few steps behind. But he had not gone far when he heard Elenna cry out.

"Get off!" she screamed.

Tom swung round, his sword drawn, expecting to see Equinus. Instead, he saw Elenna standing by a fallen log.

It looked as if she was covered in a sea of whitish slime. It was moving, starting at her ankles and working its way up her body. She was slapping wildly at her clothes.

What's going on? Tom thought. He was about to leap to her aid when he felt a crawling sensation on his legs.

He looked down to see a seething mass of huge, writhing maggots!

CHAPTER SIX

THE EVIL WIND

Tom thrashed about, brushing the horrid, squirming creatures off his clothes and skin. The maggots were a putrid, sickly white colour, and each was as big as a clenched fist. They had hungry-looking mouths.

"They're disgusting!" Elenna said, pulling at her tunic and shaking it. Some maggots fell off, but more were already crawling up from the dusty undergrowth.

"At least something is alive in this dreadful place," Tom said grimly. He quickly ran through his magical abilities in his head, but couldn't think of anything that would help get rid of the slimy creatures. "We'll just have to keep moving. That way, no more maggots will be able to climb onto us."

"Then let's go!" insisted Elenna with a shudder. "And fast. Before they decide that we might be worth eating."

They rushed through the knee-high dust, scattering the clinging maggots as they went. All the time, Tom looked this way and that for signs of Equinus.

"It doesn't make sense," said Tom, as they pushed through the decaying giant leaves and creepers of the jungle. "Why would Equinus choose to live here? Horses don't belong in jungles – even a Ghost Beast who is part-horse and part-man!"

"I suppose it's the only good place to hide for miles around," answered Elenna. She stopped suddenly and grinned. "And so it's the perfect place to hide the second piece of the amulet!"

"Of course!" exclaimed Tom. "And if we find it, I'm sure Equinus will be close by."

"I don't know," Elenna said. "But the map led us here. We have to keep going and look out for any clues that will lead us to Equinus and the amulet. And quickly."

Tom understood her urgency. Time was running out for Storm. "But it'll be like looking for a needle in a

haystack." He stared all around him.
"The amulet could be anywhere,"
he continued, and then stopped.
"Hey, wait a minute!"

They were standing by a tall tree
which so high that the top was lost
in the jungle canopy. Tom pointed at
its trunk. "Look at this!" he cried.
There were deep, crescent-shaped
grooves etched into the crumbling
bark. "These marks were made by
hooves, I'm sure of it." He stretched
up but he couldn't reach them.
"They're too far above the ground to
have been made by an ordinary
horse."

"Equinus!" said Elenna excitedly.
"It must have been. He's big enough
to reach that high. But why would
he have been kicking at this tree?"
Her brow creased with concentration,

then her eyes lit up. "Tom, remember what Aduro told us? The Beasts don't just guard the pieces of amulet – sometimes they hide them."

Tom felt himself grinning as he realised what Elenna was telling him. He turned to face her. "Equinus wasn't kicking the tree," he said. "He wanted to hide something up there, so he must have been rearing up on his hind legs and leaning his front hooves on the trunk. To go to all that effort, he must have been hiding something very precious."

"The piece of amulet!" breathed Elenna.

Tom nodded and strapped his shield to his back. "I may have lost my magical ability to leap up high," he told Elenna, "but I can still climb trees!"

He began to clamber up the trunk, but the crumbling bark made it very hard to get a grip. He gritted his teeth and pushed onwards.

"You're not the only one who can climb trees."

Tom looked down and saw Elenna following him. He was glad. He had the feeling he was going to need all the help he could get.

As they climbed, they carefully scanned the branches for any sign of the amulet. Soon the ground seemed a very long way down.

"Look, the hoofmarks don't reach this far," said Tom. "We must be at the hiding place."

"Yes, I think you're right," said Elenna. "Check the branches and the trunk – whoa!" She flung her arms tightly round the tree as it began to

shake. Tom clutched desperately at
the trunk as well.

A sudden wind had sprung up.
It circled the tree, tugging at their
clothes and making the branches
shudder. It howled and whistled with
a strange, unearthly noise.

"The wind sounds like it's laughing,"
said Elenna, as she struggled to keep
her hold on the decaying bark.

"It is laughing," Tom said, through gritted teeth. "This is no ordinary wind. I think it's been sent by Malvel to stop us." He gripped the tree even more tightly. "Blow all you like!" he shouted into the powerful breeze. "We'll never give up. We're going to find the amulet piece!"

The tree began to sway more violently, crashing against its neighbours. Branches fell about Tom's head. Bark was being stripped from under his fingers by the evil tornado, and Tom felt his feet slip. For a moment he was holding on with his arms alone. If he lost his grip he would knock into Elenna and send her plunging to the ground with him. He knew he would land safely if he fell – Arcta's eagle feather in his shield would make sure of that. But it wouldn't help Elenna. Tom searched for a foothold with the toe of his boot and, at last, found one.

"I don't know how much longer I can hold on," Elenna shouted up to him.

"You can't let go," Tom yelled back above the evil screeching roar. "We're too high. You won't survive the fa—" He broke off in shock, as Elenna seemed to suddenly lose her grip on the tree.

CHAPTER SEVEN

TERROR IN THE TREES

Tom's heart pounded fiercely in his chest, but he breathed a sigh of relief as he saw that Elenna was gripping the tree trunk tightly with her legs. She had let go with her hands so she could pull an arrow and a rope from her quiver.

"I've got an idea!" she told him quickly. "It'll keep us both safe."

She tied the rope to the feathered end of the arrow. Tom was impressed as he watched Elenna manage to tie a knot while the dreadful wind fiercely shook the tree.

"I'm going to shoot this arrow deep into that branch," she said, pointing up to a thick, sturdy limb. "Hopefully it will hold firm, and then we can tie ourselves to the rope. That way we won't fall."

"Brilliant plan!" exclaimed Tom.

Elenna pulled the bow string back and aimed the arrow at the top of the tree. The arrow shot upwards and her aim was true.

Tom gave the dangling rope a hard yank. "It's holding!" he said. "Well done, Elenna!"

He tied a loop of the rope around his waist and handed the end to his

friend so that she could do the same.
The shrieking wind was so strong
now that it seemed to snatch the
breath out of Tom's mouth as he
pulled himself up the tree. Elenna
was right behind him.

And then Tom saw a patch of
bark that looked different from the
rest of the tree – it was uneven
and protruding.

"Here!" he shouted to Elenna.
"This bit's been pulled away and then
rammed back in."

"Peel it off, Tom," she said eagerly.

Bracing himself against the wind, he worked at the bark with his fingertips. "It's coming away!" he yelled. The bark broke off and tumbled to the ground far below. Tom peered inside the hole. There, glowing brightly within the decaying tree, was a jagged piece of silver inset with blue enamel.

"It's the second piece of amulet," cried Tom in triumph. He gently put his hand into the hole and picked it up. It seemed to shine even more brightly in his grasp, although the wind threatened to pluck it away. Tom showed his precious discovery to Elenna before putting it safely in his tunic pocket.

"Let's get down," Elenna said.

Untying the rope from their waists,

they held on to the end as they bounced down the trunk in huge bounds, back to the firm, dusty jungle floor. Tom then used his super-strength to pull the rope, and the firmly embedded arrowhead fell to the ground.

Elenna tied the rope back round her waist. "Right, let's get going, " she said. "We've finished one part of our Quest, but we still have a Ghost Beast to find."

Before they had the chance to move on, they heard a terrible creak behind them and then the sound of fracturing wood. They both looked up and saw the massive tree that they'd just climbed toppling towards them.

"Watch out!" yelled Tom. They dived out of the way just as the tree hit the ground, missing them by a hair's breadth. The wind gusted madly around them for a moment and, with a final howl of fury, blew away.

The jungle was suddenly silent again. "Looks like Malvel has given up," Tom said with a grin, as he and his friend staggered to their feet. Tom reached into his pocket for the piece of amulet. Then he took hold of the leather cord round his neck, on which the first piece hung, and fitted the second piece to it.

Elenna touched his hand. "What's that on the surface?" she asked, pointing at the silver disc. There were faint lines scored into the metal. "What do you think they mean?"

Tom shook his head. "I don't know," he said. "It's one mystery that will have to wait. First, we must track down Equinus – and hope we're in time to save Storm."

"We need to head further into the rainforest," said Elenna, peering through the tightly packed trees.

Tom heard a faint sound from far away. He and Elenna froze in their tracks and listened hard. Something large and powerful was ploughing towards them through the branches and creepers of the dense jungle.

"Equinus!" whispered Elenna.

Tom nodded. "He's found us."

With a roar, the huge Ghost Beast burst out from the trees, his black heart thumping in his transparent chest. Tom and Elenna watched with horrified fascination as Equinus switched from his ghostly form to flesh-and-blood, before turning back

again with a cold shimmer. The
Beast whipped his tail viciously and
stamped his hooves, churning up the
dust all around him. The bones in
his skeletal face stood out, sharp
as knives.

His evil eyes blazed hatefully at
Tom, and he charged straight at him.

CHAPTER EIGHT

DOUBLE TROUBLE

Tom had to think quickly. Now that he had found the second piece of the amulet, he knew he must have lost another gift from the magical armour. He just didn't know which one.

"I hope I still have my super-strength," he called quickly to Elenna. "I'm going to need it. Stay here!"

Pushing his doubts aside, Tom scrambled up onto the recently fallen tree trunk. He had had an idea, but he needed to get as much height as possible if he was to stand any chance against this terrible Beast. He planted his feet as firmly as he could on the trunk, and the branches quivered and sent a shower of grey dust to the ground. With luck, the tree would hold his weight long enough for him to put his bold plan into action.

As the Beast stormed at him, Tom saw Equinus become solid once more, and his black heart disappeared under his bruised skin. Tom realised that Equinus didn't want his life force – the Beast wanted to crush him. Tom smiled to himself. This was exactly what he hoped Equinus would try to do. By becoming solid, Tom knew that he might be able to wrestle the Beast to the ground. And once he'd done that, he would find a way to plunge his sword into the black heart of the Ghost Beast.

Equinus was almost on top of him now, and at the last possible moment, Tom threw out his arms and grasped at the Beast's torso with all his might.

A terrible shock of cold stabbed through him as he fell through the Beast and crashed onto the ground.

In the instant of impact, Equinus had taken on his ghostly form once more and, as Tom had passed through him, freezing ice had made him shudder.

It took all of Tom's willpower to drag himself to his feet. The ice-cold feeling seeped through him and threatened to take over his whole body. Tom realised that, as he had passed through Equinus, the Ghost Beast had tried to take away his life force. He summoned up all his strength of heart, ignoring the trembling that shook his body as he felt his energies drain away.

Then he saw Equinus begin to turn back into solid form. This was Tom's chance! He threw himself at the Beast, wrapping his arms around his enemy's body. Some of the iciness transferred from Tom to Equinus, who gave a scream of anger and pain.

As the Beast writhed, Tom twisted
violently, using his arms to yank his
enemy's body to one side. Equinus
stumbled and fell to the ground,
dragging Tom with him.

Tom landed heavily and lay choking in the dust. His eyes streamed in the gritty air. He spotted the blurry shape of Elenna's hand coming down towards him. He grasped it gratefully and felt her pulling him to his feet. But as he wiped his eyes quickly on his sleeve, he heard a sharp, desperate howl, and saw Equinus rise up from the dust, hooves flailing.

"Look out, Elenna!" Tom shouted in warning.

Elenna staggered back, but she was looking open-mouthed at the Ghost Beast. "He's changing!"

Tom stared in disbelief. Elenna was right. Equinus was transforming, but this time not to his ghostly form. The sallow, bruised tone of his skin was changing to a faint flesh colour, which spread over his head, neck and chest. His horse body and legs were becoming a vivid, shining chestnut.

"Tom, holding on to him like that must have done something. I don't think he can turn into a ghost anymore!" exclaimed Elenna.

"My strength of heart must have given me the power to stand up to him when he tried to steal my life force," Tom replied. "Thank goodness it's not the gift I've lost."

"What do we do next?" Elenna asked.

"We fight him," Tom replied defiantly, drawing his sword. "It'll be a fairer fight now that he can't change."

But a horrible ripping noise filled the air. Before their eyes, Equinus became two separate beings. In a flash, a huge man-like creature,

covered in coarse bristles, was
standing firm on new human legs.
He was dressed in a hemp tunic. By
his side a giant horse stamped its
hooves and tossed its head wildly.
The Beast's yellow eyes flashed with
anger. It was ready to attack. Now
Tom and Elenna had two enemies
to face – and defeat – if they
were to save Storm!

The man-creature gave a roar of laughter. It was harsh, and sounded like the cracking of rock.

"Death comes in two parts!" he jeered. "Dare you to follow?" He turned and disappeared into the jungle. They heard him crashing through the undergrowth.

"You're not getting away that easily!" shouted Elenna. She gave chase. "I'll soon stop him," she yelled over her shoulder at Tom. "You deal with that horse."

Tom studied the animal. Its eyes were rolling in its head, its breath coming in panicked snorts while foam sprayed from its mouth. Tom leapt onto a nearby rock and vaulted onto its back. It reared and bucked, trying to throw him off, but Tom squeezed his legs round the horse's flanks and held on to the Beast's chestnut mane. If things continued like this, the horse would tire himself out, which was exactly what Tom wanted.

Indeed, the horse soon began to pant, and Tom gave a silent cheer of victory. But the Beast suddenly paused and then charged at a tree. A low-hanging branch rammed into Tom's midriff, sending him flying. He landed on his feet, but he was winded. He fumbled for his sword. This needed to end now. Elenna was all on her own facing the other part of the Beast.

The horse charged towards him. Raising the sword high above his head, Tom brought the hilt down against the Beast's sweating temple. With a tremendous crash, the horse collapsed into the dust, unconscious.

Now Tom had to find Elenna. He knew she was strong and brave, but Equinus was a devious Beast. He followed the trail that the Beast had left in the dust on the jungle floor. He sped between the trees, dodging huge dry leaves and clinging creepers. He tried not to think about how Storm was. All he concentrated on was destroying Equinus as soon as he could to restore his friend's life force.

Bursting through a clump of ferns, he found Elenna and Equinus. The Beast was pinned to a tree by one of her arrows. The point had gone through the hemp of his tunic and he seemed to be stuck fast. Elenna stood with another arrow, ready to fire if Equinus moved. Tom kept his sword

in his hand just in case. Elenna
didn't take her eyes off the Beast,
but she gave Tom a smile of
welcome. "I went hunting, and
look what I found," she said.

"Nice work," Tom grinned.

The sight of Tom seemed to enrage
Equinus and give him new strength.
In an instant he had torn himself free
from the tree and grabbed Elenna. He
spun her round and snatched away
her bow and arrow.

Elenna tried to wrench them back.
But with a thrust of his arm, Equinus
flung her to the ground. And before
Tom could go to her aid, the Beast
had pulled back on the bow and
was pointing an arrow directly at
Tom's heart.

CHAPTER NINE

THE FINAL BATTLE

Tom stared at the deadly sharp point of the arrow. He had never thought he would find himself facing one of his friend's weapons.

Holding the Beast's gaze and keeping his face blank to hide his intent, Tom suddenly hurled his sword through the air. The flat blade flew in an arc and smacked against the Beast's hands. With a cry of pain,

Equinus lost his grip on Elenna's bow and arrow. They fell to the ground, along with Tom's sword. Quick as lightning, Elenna snatched the weapons up and threw Tom his blade.

Equinus turned his mighty head this way and that, desperately looking for another weapon. He reached up and ripped a huge branch from the tree above. He swished it menacingly about his head.

Tom stepped forwards to face Equinus. He would fight until the end. Storm's life depended on him.

With a roar, the Beast swung his makeshift club viciously at Tom's head. Tom ducked the blow nimbly. He made a thrust with his sword, but Equinus parried it with the branch, sending a shuddering force through

Tom's arm. His enemy was strong. But as Equinus raised the branch above his head, Tom noticed sweat beads on the Beast's face. He felt hope rise inside him. Equinus was not invincible. He was finding the fight an effort.

Tom leapt aside as the branch came swinging towards him again, and he slashed at the Beast, nicking one of his bristly arms.

"Go, Tom!" Elenna yelled, but he couldn't see her now. Their fight was raising a tornado of dust around them.

The Beast was moving about clumsily in the thick, choking air. He wasn't used to being on two legs, Tom realised. *He may be stronger than me*, he thought, *but I'm more agile*.

Tom darted about the clearing, each

time avoiding the swing of the vicious club. The Beast was panting and sweating hard now as they fought. But his strength was not diminishing. He swung his weapon in front of him like a battle-axe.

Tom found himself having to jump back again and again. *I can't break through his defences,* Tom thought with frustration. An evil grin played upon the Beast's face, as if he had a secret – and as if he was sure he would win the deadly contest.

Stepping back to avoid another ferocious swipe of the branch, Tom felt his foot slip. He risked a quick look down and utter horror shot through him. He was teetering on the edge of a huge dark pit with sheer sides. Equinus had been very clever. He was pushing Tom towards the drop!

Tom struggled to keep his balance, but the ground was slipping from under his feet. Stones and earth tumbled into the pit, making no noise to show they had landed – so the pit must be bottomless. Tom knew for certain that he had no gifts to protect him from an endless fall.

With a smirk of victory, the Beast lunged at Tom, using the branch like a sword. For one terrible moment, Tom could feel that he was toppling backwards, slipping over the edge of the pit.

"Not while there's blood in my veins!" he yelled defiantly, propelling his body forwards and regaining his balance. Then he saw his chance. As Equinus lunged at him once more, he ducked beneath the branch and threw himself as hard as he could at the Beast's legs.

Now Equinus was completely off-balance. With a cry that echoed round the jungle, he stumbled over Tom's diving body and toppled headlong into the pit. As he did so, he thrust out a hand to grab Tom's ankle, but Tom rolled away from the grasping fingers.

The Beast gave a cry that became fainter and fainter as he plunged downwards. And when the dust from their fight had settled and Tom peered over the edge of the pit, he couldn't see anything – only a great, gaping black hole. Equinus had been swallowed up by the darkness.

Was his black heart gone forever?

CHAPTER TEN

SAVED!

"Tom!" Elenna rushed to his side. "Thank goodness you're all right! I couldn't see you, but I could hear the fight. It sounded terrible."

"It was," Tom said grimly. "But it's over now. With any luck, Equinus has gone for good." He hoped he was right. Then he felt a great surge of relief as the outline of a tall figure appeared in the air. "Elenna, look!"

He pointed over her shoulder. She turned, and before them stood an image of Taladon, glowing in the air. Straightaway, Tom could see that his father looked more solid.

"Well done," Taladon said, and the light around him made Tom feel warm, just as it had done before. "I cannot thank you both enough. As soon as you retrieved the piece of amulet, I felt new strength returning to me."

"The human part of Equinus has gone," said Tom. "But what about the horse? I brought him down, but I didn't see what happened after that."

"You need not fear," Taladon told him. "The horse turned to dust when you defeated Equinus's other half. You have fulfilled your Quest. But now you must make haste –

there is another who wishes to thank you."

"You mean Storm's safe?" Tom cried.

His father smiled. "Not just Storm," he said. "Anyone touched by the evil of Equinus has been returned to their former lives. Thanks to you." Taladon saluted them and his image slowly faded.

Tom felt his heart leap with joy. They had found the amulet piece and saved his beloved horse. This Quest was over.

"Let's get to Storm!" he yelled, and began to run through the trees.

"Hold on!" Elenna exclaimed. "We've gone a long way through the jungle, and I'm not sure our tracks will be clear enough to follow. Which way do we go?"

Tom held out his hand. "Map," he called. It appeared immediately in the air in front of them. Tom skidded to a halt and looked eagerly at it. A line on the ghostly map's surface materialised and showed them the way out of the jungle.

"And look. Storm's right at the end of our path!" Tom exclaimed. "Come on!"

This time Elenna didn't object. The two friends didn't stop running until they burst out onto the plain.

"There's the oak tree!" yelled Elenna.

"And there's Storm!" cried Tom happily. "And Silver!"

The two friends sprinted across the dusty earth to meet their faithful animals. Silver yelped in delight, and Tom untied Storm's reins from the tree and flung his arms round the horse's neck, before burying his face in his mane. He gazed intently into Storm's brown eyes. They were sparkling and full of life. Tom laughed with relief. Silver ran round them all, barking happily.

"Thank you, Silver," said Elenna, crouching down to greet him. "I knew we could trust you to guard Storm."

As if he understood, Silver rubbed his head against Storm's leg, and Storm put his nose down to nuzzle his friend.

Then Tom heard his father's voice in the air.

"Are you sure you are ready for your next Quest, my brave warriors?" he said.

"We are," chorused Tom and Elenna eagerly.

"Good," said Taladon's voice, and Tom could hear that his father was pleased. "Then you must journey to the Dead Peaks. Rashouk is the Beast you must fight to reclaim the next piece of the amulet. But beware – Rashouk is a troll, and one of Malvel's most terrifying Beasts. He has great cunning. You will need all your skills if you are to succeed. But there is one that I am afraid you have lost, the power granted by the golden gauntlets – your special sword skills."

With that the voice faded.

Tom stood back from Storm. "A new Beast," he murmured, fingering the pieces of amulet under his shirt. "Will I be able to defeat another of

Malvel's creatures without my sword skills?"

"You have many more skills than the magic ones you've been given," Elenna told him. "I know you can do anything you put your mind to."

Tom gave Storm a pat on the neck and turned to Elenna.

"There's only one way to find out," he declared. "On with the Quest!"

Here's a sneak preview of Tom's
next exciting adventure!

Meet

RASHOUK
THE
CAVE TROLL

Only Tom can defeat the Ghost
Beasts and save his father…

PROLOGUE

The cave was stuffy and airless, and the way ahead was blocked by a wall of stone. Fren tapped his cousin, Bly, on the shoulder. "It's a dead end," he said. "We should leave."

"We *must* find coal," Bly replied. "Winter will soon be upon us and I won't have my family going cold." He held his small, flaming torch aloft as he tapped at the wall with his pickaxe. "It's hollow," Bly smiled. "We can smash our way through."

"We'll be crossing over to the Forbidden Land," said Fren fearfully.

Bly snorted. "I don't believe those stories about the Forbidden Land!" He slipped his torch into a crevice in the cave's wall. "Besides, there might be coal on the other side."

Bly hacked at the wall and Fren helped, despite his own fears. He and Bly swung their pickaxes with matching grunts that echoed off the cave walls like flung pebbles.

Soon they were on the other side.

Fren picked up Bly's torch and cast light over the new area. "Still no coal!" he growled.

Bly opened his mouth to reply, but his voice was drowned out by a fearsome thudding sound that made the ground vibrate beneath their feet.

"We should leave!" Fren shouted, as the thudding got louder. There was a familiar rhythm to it now.

Footsteps.

From out of the shadows came a creature more terrifying than anything Fren had ever laid eyes on. The Beast wasn't much taller than a man, but was five times as wide, and his shoulders scraped along the cave walls.

Fren recognised the creature, but only from old stories he had thought were fantasy. "A troll!" he cried, stumbling backwards as the Beast pounded towards them, his yellow teeth bared. Fren could see that the troll's hands were the size of large spades, and that the fingers on his right hand had long, jagged yellow nails. "Run!" he shouted to Bly...

Follow this Quest to the end in RASHOUK THE CAVE TROLL.

Win an exclusive
Beast Quest T-shirt and goody bag!

In every Beast Quest book the Beast Quest logo is hidden
in one of the pictures. Find the logos in books 19 to 24
and make a note of which pages they appear on.
Send the six page numbers in to us.
Each month we will draw one winner to receive
a Beast Quest T-shirt and goody bag.

Send your entry on a postcard listing
the title of this book and the winning
page number to:

THE BEAST QUEST COMPETITION:
THE AMULET OF AVANTIA
Orchard Books
338 Euston Road, London NW1 3BH
Australian readers should email:
childrens.books@hachette.com.au

New Zealand readers should write to:
Beast Quest Competition
4 Whetu Place, Mairangi Bay, Auckland, NZ
or email: childrensbooks@hachette.co.nz

Only one entry per child.
Final draw: 31 May 2010

You can also enter this competition
via the Beast Quest website: www.beastquest.co.uk

Fight the Beasts,
Fear the Magic

www.beastquest.co.uk

Have you checked out the all-new Beast Quest website? It's the place to go for games, downloads, activities, sneak previews and lots of fun!

You can read all about your favourite Beast Quest monsters, download free screensavers and desktop wallpapers for your computer, and send beastly e-cards to your friends.

Sign up to the newsletter at www.beastquest.co.uk to receive exclusive extra content and the opportunity to enter special members-only competitions. It's the best place to go for up-to-date info on all the Beast Quest books, including the next exciting series, which features six brand new Beasts.

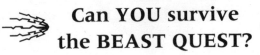Can YOU survive
the BEAST QUEST?

Read all of Tom's incredible adventures as he battles
the fearsome Beasts sent by evil Wizard Malvel.
Together with his loyal friend Elenna, his trusty
steed Storm and Silver the grey wolf, Tom risks
everything in his fight for the freedom of Avantia.

Will good conquer evil? Or will Malvel and his
Beasts destroy the kingdom? As long as there is
blood in his veins, Tom is determined to stop him...

Do BATTLE with
your friends!

Each exciting story comes with FREE collector cards!
Cut them out and play with your friends. Keep an
eye out for a special exclusive collector card – check
the Beast Quest website for details.

www.beastquest.co.uk

Series 1
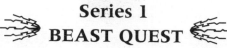
BEAST QUEST

An evil wizard has enchanted the Beasts that guard Avantia. Is Tom the hero who can free them?

978 1 84616 483 5

978 1 84616 482 8

978 1 84616 484 2

978 1 84616 486 6

978 1 84616 485 9

978 1 84616 487 3

978 1 84616 951 9

SPECIAL BUMPER EDITION!

Can Tom save the baby dragons from Malvel's evil plans?

Series 2
THE GOLDEN ARMOUR

Tom must find the pieces of the magical golden armour.
But they are guarded by six terrifying Beasts!

978 1 84616 988 5

978 1 84616 989 2

978 1 84616 990 8

978 1 84616 991 5

978 1 84616 992 2

978 1 84616 993 9

978 1 84616 994 6

Will Tom find Spiros
in time to save his
aunt and uncle?